Repaired 6/16,

Contents

A.J.
RYAN
MICHAEL
ANDREA
EMILY
NEIL

CANDY
Deluxe
CANDY

1 Tomorrow Isn't Now

My name is A.J., and I hate October 30.

If you ask me, October 30 is the worst day of the year. You know why? Because I'm not allowed to eat any candy on that day. We have these giant bags of candy all over the house, and my mom won't let me touch them.

"No candy, A.J.!" she always says on

October 30. "That candy is for the trick-or-treaters."

"Oh, come on, Mom! Can I have just one piece?"

"No! You can have all the candy you want tomorrow."

"Yeah, but tomorrow isn't *now*!"

I hate tomorrow. Tomorrow is the worst day of the week, because it isn't here yet. Waiting for tomorrow feels like forever.

The good thing is, tomorrow is also the *best* day of the week, because the day after the worst day of the year is the best day of the year: Halloween! You can eat all the candy you want, and nobody can stop you!

The other reason I don't like October

30 is because it's Mischief Night. Teenagers in our town go around throwing eggs, soaping up windows, ringing doorbells, and doing other mean stuff.

At seven o'clock I went to peek out the front window to make sure our house was safe. And you'll never believe in a million hundred years what I saw outside.

Our trees were covered with toilet paper!

Somebody TP'd our house! Can you believe that? What a mean thing to do! And I knew exactly who did it, too.

Andrea Young.

She is this girl with curly brown hair in my class at school.* It *had* to be Andrea!

---

*Well, she has curly brown hair *wherever* she goes.

She hates me. Last year me and the guys TP'd *her* house. Now she was getting me back.

Well, two can play at *that* game, Andrea. Revenge will be mine, and revenge will be sweet.

2

My Secret Plan

I grabbed a bar of soap from our bathroom sink. My secret plan was to go over to Andrea's house and soap up her windows. That would show her who's boss. Nobody TP's *my* house and gets away with it.

I knew that my mom would never let me go out so late to soap up Andrea's windows. I would have to come up with another reason to get out of the house.

"Mom, can I go over to Ryan's house for a few minutes?" I asked. "I need to get our homework assignment for tonight."

"Okay," she said, "but why do you have a bar of soap in your hand?"

"Uh . . . I may have to wash my hands," I lied.

"A.J., I'm *sure* Ryan has soap at his house."

"I don't like Ryan's soap," I told her. "It smells stinky."

"Why don't you just wash your hands right here and *then* go over to Ryan's house?" Mom asked.

"My hands might get dirty while I'm over there," I explained. "Ryan's house is really filthy."

"Just *go,* A.J.," my mom said as she rubbed her forehead with her fingers.

Yes! I win! If you can get your mom or dad to rub their forehead with their fingers, they'll agree to just about *anything.* That's the first rule of being a kid.

Ryan lives down the street from me. I ran over to his house as fast as I could so I wouldn't be attacked by any monsters along the way. You never know when there might be monsters out, roaming the streets.

I told Ryan my secret plan to soap up

Andrea's windows. He told his mom that he needed to go to my house to get tonight's homework assignment. It took some convincing, but finally she rubbed her forehead with her fingers and said he could go. Little did she know that we were going to Andrea's house to do a little mischief.

Ryan and I sneaked down the street like secret agents, hiding behind cars and trees so we wouldn't get caught. It was cool.

"I'm traveling incognito," I whispered to Ryan.

"What's a cognito?"

"How should I know?" I said. "But secret

agents always travel in them."*

After walking a million hundred miles, we finally reached Andrea's street.

"This is gonna be *great*!" Ryan whispered.

"Shhhhhhh!"

We crept up to Andrea's front window.

---

*It means "in disguise." See, you actually *learned* something from this book. So this isn't just a dumb story. It's *educational*!

I reached into my pocket.

I took out the bar of soap.

And just as I was about to rub the soap all over the window, I saw the most horrible, revolting, disgusting creature I have ever encountered in my life.

It was Andrea!

"Ahhhhhhh!" Ryan and I screamed.

"What are *you* doing over here, Arlo?" asked Andrea as she lifted up the window. She calls me by my real name because she knows I don't like it.

"Uh . . . nothing," I said. "We were, uh . . . bird-watching."

"Yeah," Ryan agreed. "We were watching birds. I think I just saw a yellow-bellied sapsucker in that tree over there."

"You were going to soap up my windows!" Andrea said, pointing her finger at me.

"Who, me?" I said. "Don't be ridiculous! I would never do a thing like that."

"You would too, Arlo!"

"Would not!"

"Would too!"

We went back and forth like that for a while.

"If you didn't come over here to soap up my windows, then what are you doing standing outside my window with soap in your hand?" Andrea demanded. "Arlo, this is probably the first time you ever used soap in your *life*."

"Oh, snap!" said Ryan. "She just said you're a dirty, disgusting pig. But not in those words. Are you gonna take that, A.J.?"

"You TP'd my house!" I said, pointing my finger at Andrea.

"I did not!"

"You did too!"

We went back and forth like that for a while, until Andrea turned around and started shouting to her parents.

"Mom! Dad! Some creepy boys are outside on the front lawn!"

"Run for it!" I shouted to Ryan.

We bolted out of there as fast as we could go.

The Gang's All Here

I never did get to soap up Andrea's windows that night. But it was okay. Because the next morning it was Halloween. The *best* day of the year!

At school, Mr. Granite was trying to teach us all kinds of stuff, but I wasn't paying attention. I couldn't concentrate on anything he was saying. All I could think about was candy. I couldn't wait for the bell to ring. It felt like the clock was going backward.

But finally it was three o'clock. I ran home to put on my Halloween costume.

In our town, you're not allowed to start trick-or-treating until four o'clock in the afternoon. Bummer in the summer! I would have to wait even *longer* to get the candy.

Me and the gang had decided we would all combine two or more things together in our costumes. I had an old *Star Wars* costume in the closet, and my sister, Amy, let me use the deer costume she wore last year. So this Halloween I was going to be . . .

Darth Bambi!

Pretty good, huh? No wonder I'm in the gifted and talented program.

One by one, the gang came over so we could all go trick-or-treating together.

"Who are *you*?" my mother asked everybody as they came to the door.

"I'm a flying robot ninja from outer space," said Michael, who never ties his shoes.

"I'm a mutant zombie pirate," said Ryan, who will eat anything, even stuff that isn't food.

"I'm a skateboarding hippie dinosaur,"

said Alexia, who skateboards everywhere she goes.

Next came Neil, who we call the nude kid even though he wears clothes. None of us had any idea what he was dressed up as.

"I'm a flying mutant pirate hobo ninja robot dinosaur," said Neil, "from outer space."

That's just *too* much stuff.

"We're traveling incognito," I told my mom.

"*Ooooo*, you all look so *spooky*!" my mom said.

That's when the most amazing thing in the history of the world happened.

The doorbell rang.

Well, that's not the amazing part, because doorbells ring all the time. The amazing part was what happened *next*.

"A.J., answer the door, please," my mother said. "It must be our first trick-or-treater. I'll get the candy."

But it wasn't our first trick-or-treater. It was my friend Billy, who lives around the corner. Billy goes to another school. I invited him to go trick-or-treating with us.

The amazing part was that when I opened the door, Billy was standing there in his *underwear*! You should have been there. It was hilarious. Anything to do with underwear is hilarious. That's the first rule of being a kid.

"*That's* your costume, Billy?" my mom asked with her hands on her hips.

"You've heard of the werewolf," said Billy. "Well, I'm the *under*werewolf! *Grrrrrrr!*"

He made scary noises and posed like a werewolf. It was still hilarious. It's hard to look scary when you're in your underwear.

The fact is, Billy goes as the underwerewolf *every* Halloween. If you ask me, Billy just likes to parade around in his underwear.

Billy's weird.

It was a quarter to four. We couldn't go

trick-or-treating yet, so we went into the den to fool around with my dad's computer. I wanted to go on YouTube and watch videos of cats playing the piano, but Michael had another idea. He went to Google Maps and typed in the address of my house.

"Okay, here's my plan for maximum candy accumulation," Michael said as he moved his finger across the screen. "People on Maple Street give out the best candy, so we should head over there first. Then we can turn left on Pine Street and hit Hickory, Elm, and Sycamore Street. The people on Evergreen Avenue never have any good candy, so we should skip that street. . . ."

Michael is a genius when it comes to trick-or-treating strategy. After he was finished plotting our route, we printed out the map so we wouldn't get lost.

It was a few minutes before four o'clock. My mom gave us old pillowcases we could use to hold our candy. Billy gathered us all around him like a football team in a huddle.

"Okay, dudes," he said. "What do we want?"

"Candy!" we all shouted.

"I can't *hear* you! What do we want?"

"CANDY!" we shouted louder.

"When do we want it?" Billy asked.

"Now!"

"How much candy do we want?" Billy asked.

"A lot!"

"Where do we want it?" Billy asked.

"In our mouths!" we shouted. "In our tummies!"

"That's right!" Billy said. "This is going to be the greatest Halloween in the history of the world!"

The clock in the hall struck four.

"It's time!" we all screamed as we charged out the door. "Let's go! Candy! Candy! Candy!"

4 The Rules of Halloween

We followed Michael's map until we came to the first house on Maple Street. We all ran up the front steps. Alexia rang the doorbell. A bald guy opened the door.

"Oob!" we all shouted.

"Oob?" the bald guy said. "Don't you mean boo?"

"'Oob' is 'boo' backward," I told him.

Saying stuff backward is cool.*

"Treat or trick!" yelled Ryan.

"I guess you mean trick or treat," the

*"Cool" backward is "looc." "Stuff" backward is "ffuts." "Backward" backward is "drawkcab."

bald guy said. "Well, what's the trick?"

We all looked at each other. Nobody knew any tricks. It had never come up before. People always gave us candy, no questions asked. Maybe this guy just came to America a few days ago, and he didn't know how Halloween worked yet.

"You're supposed to give us candy," I explained to the guy. "Then we leave."

"What if I don't have any candy?" the guy asked. "You're supposed to play a trick on me."

"We don't have any tricks," Neil told him.

"Well, I don't have any candy," the guy replied.

"How can you not have candy?" asked Alexia. "It's *Halloween.*"

"Yeah, don't you know the rules of Halloween, mister?" I asked.

"I ate all my candy yesterday," the guy told us. "I have a sweet tooth, and I couldn't resist."

Some people just don't get Halloween. I bet that guy had plenty of candy, but he just wanted to give us a hard time. I'm not sure I would want his candy anyway.

We got out of there fast. That guy was weird.

5 Ghosts, Goblins, and Ghouls

"Oob!" we shouted when we came to the next house. "Treat or trick!"

The old lady who answered the door was wearing an apron. She held out a big basket full of candy.

"You can each take one," she said.

"Can I take two?" Ryan asked.

"Okay, okay, you can take two," she agreed.

"Can I take *three*?" I asked.

"No."

That lady was mean.

We went up and down Maple Street, grabbing fistfuls of Kit Kats, M&M'S, Smarties, Warheads, Hershey's bars, Jolly Ranchers, Life Savers, Reese's Pieces, York Peppermint Patties, Mounds, Jelly Bellies. . . .

Well, you get the idea.

I wanted to start eating my candy right away, but Michael and Billy said we should get a whole bunch of candy before we started eating any of it. After we cleaned out all the houses on Maple Street, we moved on to Pine Street.

"My pillowcase is getting heavy!" complained Alexia.

"Mine too," agreed Neil the nude kid.

"I say we should eat some of our candy

now," suggested Ryan. "Then our pillowcases won't feel so heavy."

What a genius! We could eat candy and lighten our pillowcases at the *same time.* Ryan should get the No Bell Prize for that idea. That's a prize they give out to people who don't have bells.

We stopped on the corner and took a break. I had a Laffy Taffy. Ryan had a Mars bar. Billy had a Snickers. Michael had some Tootsie Rolls. Neil had some Starburst. Yum!

I still can't get over the fact that on Halloween people just hand you candy, and you don't even have to pay for it or anything. What a scam! We all agreed that Halloween is the best holiday of all the holidays, and this was the greatest day of our lives.

By now the streets were filled with lots of kids out trick-or-treating. We saw some pretty scary-looking costumes. There were kids dressed like ghosts, goblins, ghouls, zombies, and hunchbacks.

I saw these two kids who were *really* scary. One of them didn't have a head, and the other one had *two* heads! That was weird.* But right after that, I saw the most hideous, horrifying creature in the history of the world.

It was Andrea Young!

Ugh, disgusting! She was walking toward us. And she was with her crybaby friend Emily. Just once I wish I could go someplace without bumping into *those* two.

"I'm a witch," Andrea announced, as if

---

*But not really, because they averaged out to one head for each of them.

we couldn't figure it out from the pointy hat, broomstick, and wart on her nose. She spun around so we could see her costume in all its glory.

"You look even uglier than usual," I told Andrea.

"Oh, snap!" said Ryan.

"I'm a witch too," said Emily, who always does everything Andrea does.

"We're good witches, not bad witches," Andrea informed us.

"You should put bread on either side of you," I suggested. "Then you'd be a sandwich."

"Very funny, Arlo," Andrea said, rolling her eyes.

“I’m a mutant zombie pirate,” said Ryan. *“Arghhhh!”*

“I’m the *under*werewolf!” said Billy. *“Grrrrrrr!”*

"My mom told me that violent costumes are inappropriate for children," Andrea said. "They could lead to violent behavior."

"Your mom is weird," I told Andrea.

"Look," Michael said. "We don't have time to make chitchat with you two. There's a lot of candy out there, and we want to go get it."

"Oh, I don't care about getting a lot of candy," Andrea told us. "I'm going to donate any candy I collect to the poor. There are a lot of children who can't afford candy."

"They don't *have* to afford candy!" Alexia said. "It's free!"

"Yeah," I said. "They can go out on the street and get it, just like us!"

"That's not the point, Arlo," Andrea said. "The point is to help people. Hey, why don't you join us, and we'll donate *all* our candy to poor people?"

"Are you *crazy*?" Neil said. "We're keeping our candy. The candy we get tonight is going to last us all year."

"Yeah," said Michael, showing Andrea the map he made. "We have a plan for maximum candy accumulation."

"That's too bad," said Andrea. "This morning I was in the computer room at school, and Mrs. Yonkers told me to make sure I come and trick-or-treat at her house. She said she would have a magical Halloween surprise treat that we couldn't get anywhere else in the world."

WHAT!? A magical Halloween surprise treat that we couldn't get anywhere else in the world?

I looked at Michael. Michael looked at Ryan. Ryan looked at Alexia. Alexia looked at Neil. Neil looked at Billy. Billy looked at me.

In case you were wondering, we were all looking at each other.

"Let's go!" we shouted.

6 The Halloween Monster

We all followed Andrea so we could go to Mrs. Yonkers's house and get the magical Halloween surprise treat. She made a left at Avondale Avenue. Then she made a right at Redman Road. Then she made a left at West End Street.

Those streets weren't on Michael's map. I didn't know where we were anymore.

Andrea looked a little confused. It seemed like she didn't know where she was either.

"Where does Mrs. Yonkers live anyway?" I asked her.

"I know her house is around here *somewhere*," Andrea said. "Maybe it's down this street."

But it wasn't down that street. And it wasn't down the next street either. We passed by a big field. The houses were getting farther apart.

We must have walked a million hundred miles. We didn't find Mrs. Yonkers's house, and we weren't even getting candy anymore. This wasn't fun at all. The sun was going down. Soon it would be dark out.

Suddenly, Andrea stopped.

"I'm lost," she admitted.

"Lost?" asked Emily. She looked like she was going to cry.

"I don't know which way to go," said Andrea. "I'm scared."

To be honest with you, I was a little scared myself.

But part of me was happy that we were lost. In school, Little Miss Know-It-All never makes any mistakes. She's always in control of everything. Now we were lost, and it was all Andrea's fault. Ha! It was kind of fun to watch her freak out for a change.

"Y'know," I said, "this is just the kind of neighborhood where the Halloween

Monster would be hiding."

"Halloween Monster?" asked Emily, her eyes wide open.

"You never heard of the Halloween Monster?" I asked her. "He lives in a cave, and he only comes out on Halloween. Every year on this night, he sneaks up from behind, chops kids into little pieces, steals their candy, and keeps it for himself. Stuff like that happens all the time, you know."

I was totally yanking Emily's chain. There was no such thing as a Halloween Monster. I just made it up.

"Arlo, stop trying to scare Emily," Andrea said.

"I'm scared!" said Emily.

"Dudes, we need to get out of here," Billy said. "We could be stranded in the middle of nowhere for the rest of our lives."

"At least we have something to eat so we can survive," Ryan said. "I think we should eat some candy so we don't starve to death."

"Didn't we just eat some candy five minutes ago?" asked Neil.

"I think Ryan has a good idea," I said, grabbing a Milky Way out of my pillowcase.

Any idea that involves eating candy is a good idea, if you ask me. That's the first rule of being a kid.

"I'm not hungry," said Alexia.

"Me neither," said Michael.

"Well, I am," said Billy.

"I'm saving my candy for later," said Neil.

We went back and forth like that for a while. But as we were arguing over when to eat our candy, something had sneaked up behind us.

I heard a noise.

I turned around.

And standing before us was a giant, six-foot creature that was covered with brown fur from head to toe.

"Your candy or your life!" the horrible thing said with a growl.

It was the Halloween Monster!

7

Sugar Shock

The Halloween Monster was *real*!

I thought I was gonna die. The disgusting, horrifying creature was standing a foot away from me, staring at me with his beady monster eyes. He was holding open a big black garbage bag.

I didn't know what to say. I didn't know

what to do. I had to think fast. But I was frozen.*

"Did you hear me?" the Halloween

*But not like a Popsicle or an ice cube or anything like that.

Monster barked at me. "Your candy or your life!"

"I'm thinking, I'm thinking," I said.

It was a hard decision. If I gave the Halloween Monster all my candy, I wouldn't have any candy left, but I would still have my life. I had to ask myself, is life really worth living without candy?

And if I gave him my life, I would still have my candy; but I wouldn't be able to eat it, because I would be dead.

I was faced with the toughest decision in the history of the world. I was thinking so hard that my brain hurt. Why is making decisions so complicated?

In the end it didn't matter *what* I decided,

because everybody else rushed forward to dump their candy into the bag that the Halloween Monster was holding. Then he grabbed my pillowcase from my hand and dumped all my candy into his bag.

"Hey! That's *my* candy!" I yelled at him.

But he didn't care. The Halloween Monster ran down the street with all our candy.

This was the worst thing to happen since TV Turnoff Week! It was the worst thing to happen since National Poetry Month!

It took a few minutes for us to calm down after the Halloween Monster ran away.

"That was *mean*!" Alexia yelled. "Why

would somebody steal candy from kids?"

"Just be thankful that he didn't chop us up into little pieces," said Ryan.

"Wow," I said, "I didn't know the Halloween Monster was real. I just thought he was a pigment of my imagination."

"That's 'figment,' dumbhead," Andrea said. "Pigment is what they use to make paint."

"They should put paint on your *face*," I told Andrea.

What is her problem? Why can't a truck full of paint fall on Andrea's head?

"It wasn't a monster," said Michael. "It was just some grown-up disguised as a monster."

"He's traveling in a cognito," Ryan said.

"What's a cognito?" asked Billy.

"It's what secret agents travel in," Ryan told him.

We were all depressed, because we had worked so hard to get that candy and now it was gone. We would have to start all over again. Bummer in the summer!

We turned the corner and went to the first house on that street and got some candy there. Then we hit another house. Soon we were back in the groove, scooping up candy left and right and filling up our pillowcases with it as we made our way down the street.

"Y'know, we should start eating some

of this candy now," Ryan suggested. "That way the Halloween Monster won't be able to get it."

"Good point, dude," said Billy. "Nobody can steal our candy if we eat it."

"I'm not eating mine," said Alexia. "I'd rather save some for a rainy day."

"What does the weather have to do with eating candy?" I asked her. "I'm hungry *now*."

"My mother told me that if you eat too much candy, you'll get sick," Andrea said. "You could go into sugar shock."

Nobody tells *me* how much candy I can eat. And I'm sure not going to listen to a smarty-pants know-it-all like Andrea. I stuffed a 3 Musketeers bar into my mouth and swallowed it in one gulp.

"Oh, yeah?" said Ryan. "Watch *this*!"

Ryan unwrapped two Twix bars and shoved them into his face. It didn't even look like he chewed them.

"WOW," everybody said, which is "MOM" upside down.

Then Michael took *three* Hershey's bars out of his pillowcase. He ripped the wrappings off them, stacked them like pancakes, and ate all *three* of them at the same time. It was amazing!

Nobody can eat more candy than *me*. I took a giant Butterfinger and swallowed it. We all started furiously unwrapping candy bars and stuffing them into our faces as fast as we could. All of us except for Andrea and Emily, of course.

It was like one of those eating contests on Coney Island where guys eat fifty hot dogs one after the other. We were eating our candy like it was the last day on Earth before a meteorite destroyed the planet.

You should have been there! It was the greatest day of my life.

Andrea and Emily just watched us, rolling their eyes and saying how disgusting we were.

After a few million hundred candy bars, my stomach was starting to feel a little funny. For the first time in my life, I didn't

want to eat any more candy. All I wanted to do was lie down.

That's when everything went black.

8
Nightmare of the Living Teachers

Spooky music was playing, but I couldn't tell where it was coming from. The whole world around me was dark and gloomy. I didn't know if I was awake or asleep. It was *creepy*.

"Where am I?" I asked. "Is this a dream . . . or a nightmare?"

But nobody answered.

And then I heard the sound of footsteps. Lots of footsteps. They were getting closer. Coming toward me.

"Help!" I tried to shout. "Help!"

But no words came out of my mouth.

Soon I was able to make out some faces. I was surrounded by people coming at me from all sides.

They were the teachers at my school!

Mrs. Daisy! Mrs. Roopy! Mr. Granite! Ms. Hannah! Mr. Macky! Miss Small! They were *all* there! And they were wearing weird costumes. They had their hands out in front of them and glassy looks in their eyes. It was like I was being attacked by zombie teachers!

"We're coming to get you, A.J." they droned. "We're coming to get you. . . ."

"Noooooooooooo!"

I tried to back away from them, but there was a wall behind me. The teachers were all over me.

"Candy rots your teeth," said Mrs. Cooney, our school nurse. "We must take it away from you."

"Candy spoils your appetite," said Ms. LaGrange, our lunch lady. "We must take it away from you."

"Candy is bad for you," said Miss Holly, our Spanish teacher. "We must take it away from you."

"No! No!" I shouted. "Don't take my

candy away! Please! I'm begging you!"

"Okay," said Ms. Hannah, our art teacher. "Then we're going to pour green paint all over you."

"What? Wait! Why?"

"It's my favorite color," Ms. Hannah said as she dumped a big bucket filled with green paint all over my head.

"No! Stop! Don't!"

"Aha-ha-ha!" yelled Ms. Hannah. "It's Halloween! He's turning green!"

All the teachers started chanting.

"He's turning green! It's Halloween! He's turning green!"

"HELLLLLLLLLLLLLLLPPPPPPPPP!"

But they wouldn't stop. My whole body

was covered with green paint. I couldn't see. I couldn't hear. It was the worst dream I ever had. I hoped it was a dream anyway.

Suddenly, the teachers stopped pouring green paint on me. They turned around. They looked frightened.

"Run!" shouted Mr. Klutz, our principal. "Quickly! Run away!"

The teachers ran away, and you'll never believe in a million hundred years who showed up a few seconds later. It was a group of penguins! There must have been hundreds of them! Or was it a bunch of little kids dressed up like penguins? I wasn't sure.

"Come with us, A.J.," one of the penguins said. "Come with us to Antarctica."

They looked like they were friendly penguins.

"Penguins can talk?" I asked.

"Of course," said one of the other penguins.

"In Antarctica there are no mean

teachers who steal your candy or pour green paint over you," a penguin said. "Just lots of nice, clean snow and ice."

"Yes, and candy," said another penguin.

"We can play in the snow and eat candy all day long," said the first penguin. "All the candy you can eat. And you'll never get sick."

"Really?" I asked. "Antarctica sounds *wonderful*."

"It will be like Halloween every day of the year," said another penguin. "Come with us, A.J. Come with us to Antarctica. It's right around the corner."

"Right around the corner . . . ," I mumbled. "Halloween every day . . ."

9 A Bunch of Squirrels

"Wake up! Dude, are you okay?"

I opened my eyes. Billy was kneeling over me.

"Huh? What? Where am I?" I asked.

The whole gang was standing there in a circle around me: Ryan, Michael, Alexia, Neil, Andrea, Emily. I checked my arms and legs. They were clean. I didn't have any green paint on me.

"You must have had some kind of a nightmare, dude," Billy said. "You were *out.* We thought we might have to call an ambulance."

"You kept mumbling something about

going around the corner," said Ryan.

"The teachers at school were trying to steal my candy," I told them. "They were walking around like zombies. All of them! When I refused to give them the candy, they dumped green paint all over me."

"Paint?" asked Neil.

"I guess it wasn't *real* paint," I said. "It was just a pigment of my imagination."

"That was scary!" said Emily, who's scared by just about anything.

"Why would the teachers want to dump green paint on you?" Alexia asked. "That doesn't make any sense."

"It was a dream!" I told her. "Dreams don't always make sense. It was horrible!

But then I was rescued by some nice penguins. They wanted me to run away with them to Antarctica."

"You should have listened to me, Arlo," Andrea told me. "I *told* you that eating so much candy would make you sick."

"Your *face* makes me sick," I told Andrea.

"Oh, snap!" said Ryan.

I got up off the ground and brushed the dirt off my costume.

"That was one weird dream you had, dude," Billy said. "Maybe you should stop eating so much candy."

As it turned out, I *had* to stop eating so much candy, because my pillowcase had nothing in it except for candy wrappers. I had eaten all my candy! Ryan and Michael said they only had a few candy bars left. The only ones who had a lot of candy were Andrea and Emily.

It was dark out, and it was getting late. Soon trick-or-treating would be over, and we would have to go home. Bummer in the summer!

"Hey," Ryan suddenly said, "if I go home without any candy, I won't have any candy to eat tomorrow."

"That's right," agreed Michael. "The only candy we have in our house is Halloween candy."

"Same here," said Neil the nude kid. "I might have to wait a whole year until next

Halloween before I can get more candy."

This was a *horrible* situation!

"What are we going to do?" asked Alexia.

There was only one thing we *could* do.

"Get more candy!" we all shouted.

We took off down the street, knocking on every door we could find. When we finished the street, we turned down the next street and went trick-or-treating there. I didn't even know which direction we were heading in anymore. I didn't care. I just wanted to fill my pillowcase with candy. We were like a bunch of squirrels, gathering nuts so we would be able to make it through the winter.

Finally, after a million hundred minutes, we had lots of candy again. There was one more house on the street that we hadn't visited. We all ran up the front steps.

"Hey, wait a minute," Andrea said, checking the number on the front porch. "I know who lives in this house! You'll never believe who it is."

"Who?" we all shouted.

"Mrs. Yonkers!"

10 The Expanding Universe

Andrea rang the doorbell, and sure enough Mrs. Yonkers popped her head out of the screen door.

Well, she didn't *really* pop her head out of the screen door. If you popped your head out of a screen door, it would hurt. Also, you wouldn't have a head anymore.

"Oob!" we all shouted. "Treat or trick!"

"Well, howdy, y'all!" Mrs. Yonkers said. "Yee-ha! I've been waiting for you varmints to show up."

She's from Texas. People from Texas say "y'all," "yee-ha," and "varmints" all the time on TV. Nobody knows why.

Mrs. Yonkers is the computer teacher at our school. She's a genius, and she's always inventing stuff. Like one time she invented a giant hamster wheel that generated electricity. Another time she invented a boat that traveled through time. She even started her own computer company called NERD: New Electronic Research Development.

Mrs. Yonkers was wearing one of those big yellow fake-cheese hats. It wasn't her Halloween costume. She wears that thing all the time. Nobody knows why. She let each of us take two candy bars from her bowl.

"Andrea said you have a magical Halloween surprise treat that we can't get anywhere else," I said.

"I do!" Mrs. Yonkers told us. "Do y'all want to see it?"

"Yee-ha!" we all shouted.

Everybody was excited as Mrs. Yonkers led us into her kitchen. She told us she had created a top secret invention that nobody knew about yet. Then she waved her hand dramatically and pointed to the microwave oven.

"Ta-da!" she said. "Here it is!"

We all looked at it.

"Uh, that's just a microwave oven," Ryan said.

"Oh, it *looks* just like a microwave oven," Mrs. Yonkers told us. "But actually, it's the revolutionary new MicroMole 4000 Expandinator."

We all looked at it some more. It sure looked like a microwave oven to me.

"What does it do?" asked Neil the nude kid.

"Let me see if I can explain," Mrs. Yonkers told us. "For thousands of years, scientists have wondered where the universe ends. Does it have an edge somewhere, or does it just go on forever and ever?"

"What does that have to do with your machine?" Billy asked.

"You'll see," Mrs. Yonkers replied. "In

1929, an astronomer named Edwin Hubble proved that the universe is expanding all the time.* With the MicroMole 4000 Expandinator, I figured out how to accelerate the rate of expansion by altering the molecular structure and blah blah blah blah blah blah blah blah blah blah blah blah blah blah blah blah blah blah blah . . ."

Mrs. Yonkers went on like that for a while. It didn't seem like the universe was expanding to me, but it sounded like a cool idea. If the universe was expanding, maybe there would be more video games

---

*This is actually true. Go look it up if you don't believe me.

and skate parks.

Finally, Mrs. Yonkers finished talking about the universe expanding.

"So what does the MicroMole 4000 Expandinator actually *do*?" asked Andrea.

"Oh, that's simple," Mrs. Yonkers told us. "It makes stuff bigger."

WHAT?!!!

"You mean to say that if you put something in that machine and turn it on, it makes the thing *bigger*?" asked Ryan.

"That's right," said Mrs. Yonkers. "See for yourself."

She picked up a pot holder from the kitchen counter and put it inside the MicroMole 4000 Expandinator. Then she pushed a button. The machine turned on and made a noise just like a microwave oven. About ten seconds later, there was a little *ding* sound. Mrs. Yonkers opened up the MicroMole 4000 Expandinator. And you'll never believe in a million hundred years what was inside.

A GIANT POT HOLDER!

"WOW," we all shouted, which is "MOM" upside down.

"That's *amazing*!" Andrea said. "It's like the universe expanded in the machine!"

She was right. That is, if the universe was only made up of pot holders.

"Will the MicroMole 4000 Expandinator work with other objects too?" asked Michael.

"It will work with anything."

"Will it work with candy?" I asked.

"Sure!" said Mrs. Yonkers.

She picked a Hershey's bar out of her bowl and put it in the MicroMole 4000 Expandinator. Ten seconds after she turned the machine on, she opened the door and took out the Hershey's bar.

It was the size of a cereal box!

"Gasp!" we all gasped.

"That is the greatest invention in the history of the world," I said. "You should get the No Bell Prize, Mrs. Yonkers."

"Oh, I don't care about prizes," she told us. "But think of how the MicroMole 4000 Expandinator could be used. It could help poor people get enough food to feed a large family. It could help people with vision problems to see tiny objects. The possibilities are unlimited."

Personally, all I cared about was getting some *really* big candy. Mrs. Yonkers said we could take our bite-size Halloween candy, put it in the MicroMole 4000 Expandinator, and turn it into GIANT, FAMILY-SIZE CANDY. We did it, and it was the coolest thing *ever*! When we were finished, I could barely lift my pillowcase full of giant, expanded candy.

"Thanks, Mrs. Yonkers!" we all said.

"Now remember," she told us. "The MicroMole 4000 Expandinator is a top

secret project. Nobody knows about it yet except for us. So not a word to anyone, okay?"

"Our lips are sealed," Andrea said.*

---

*But not really. It would be weird if your lips were sealed. How would you talk? How would you sneeze? How would you brush your teeth?

We were about to turn around to leave when the most amazing thing in the history of the world happened. I felt the presence of someone else in the room.

"Not so fast!" a voice shouted.

We all turned around.

It was the Halloween Monster again!

11

The Return of the Halloween Monster

"Ahhhhhhhhhh!" we all screamed.

"It's the Halloween Monster!"

That big, ugly, disgusting, furry Halloween Monster was standing right in front of us! He must have followed us to Mrs. Yonkers's house.

"Run for your lives!" shouted Neil the nude kid.

But there was no place to run. There was no place to hide. We were trapped in the kitchen. Emily was on the floor, freaking out. For once I couldn't blame her. We were *all* freaking out.

"Who are you?" Mrs. Yonkers yelled at the Halloween Monster. "Get out of my house, you varmint! I didn't invite you in here."

"Take our candy!" I shouted. "Go ahead. I don't want it. Just don't chop us up into little pieces. Please!"

"I don't want your dumb candy," the Halloween Monster said angrily.

"What do you want then?" asked Andrea.

"I want . . . the MicroMole 4000 Expandinator!" the Halloween Monster shouted.

WHAT?!

"No!" Mrs. Yonkers yelled, wrapping her arms around the MicroMole 4000 Expandinator. "This is *my* invention!"

"But soon it will be *mine*," said the Halloween Monster. "Think of it. I could build a larger version of your machine. Then I could take solid gold coins and turn them into solid gold *manhole covers*! I could take a compact car and turn it into an SUV! I could climb inside the MicroMole 4000 Expandinator and supersize myself. I would become a *giant*! With this technology, I could . . . rule the world! Aha-ha-ha-ha-ha!"

The Halloween Monster let out an evil, cackling laugh. He was obviously crazy. Any time somebody says they want to rule the world and they let out an evil, cackling laugh, you know they're nuts.

"Get out of here before I call the police, you varmint!" shouted Mrs. Yonkers as she reached for the phone with one hand.

"First hand over the MicroMole 4000 Expandinator," said the Halloween Monster.

"Never!" yelled Mrs. Yonkers.

"Don't make this difficult, lady," said the Halloween Monster. "Just give me the machine, and nobody will get hurt."

"No way!"

"You heard her," I yelled at the Halloween Monster. "Get out of here! She's not going to give it to you."

"Oh, well," he said, "then I guess I'm just going to have to *take* it."

He reached out to grab the MicroMole 4000 Expandinator from Mrs. Yonkers's hands. She held on tight.

The Halloween Monster got hold of the MicroMole 4000 Expandinator!

Mrs. Yonkers grabbed it back!

Then the two of them were wrestling on the floor and yelling at each other!

Watching grown-ups wrestle is cool.

And we got to see it live and in person. You should have been there!

And then, suddenly, the most amazing thing in the history of the world happened. Two men burst in the front door. They were wearing policeman costumes.

"Freeze, dirtbag!" they hollered at the Halloween Monster.

Cops on TV always shout "Freeze, dirtbag" at bad guys. Nobody knows why.

Everybody froze.

But not really. It would have had to be really cold in Mrs. Yonkers's house for everybody to freeze.

"Step away from the machine, mister," said one of the guys dressed up as a policeman. "Put your hands in the air."

The Halloween Monster stepped away from the MicroMole 4000 Expandinator and put his hands up.

"Hey, those are great costumes," I said. "I've never seen a trick-or-treater dressed up as a policeman before."

"They're not dressed up like policemen, Arlo!" Andrea said, rolling her eyes. "They're *real* policemen."

Oh. I knew that.

"My name is Officer Harwell," one of the policemen said, "and this is Officer Trotta. We got a report that there was a man going around town stealing candy from kids. We followed him to this address."

"I didn't steal any candy!" hollered the Halloween Monster.

"Has this man been stealing candy?" asked Officer Trotta.

"Yes!" we all shouted. "He stole it from us!"

"You're under arrest," Officer Harwell said to the Halloween Monster. "You have the right to remain silent. Anything you say will be used against you blah blah blah blah blah blah blah blah."

He went on like that for a while.

"Remove the head of your costume, sir," said Officer Trotta. "We need to be sure you don't have a concealed weapon in there."

We all gathered around because we wanted to see the true identity of the Halloween Monster. As he started to take off the head of his costume, we were all on pins and needles.

Well, not really. If we were on pins and needles, it would have hurt. But it was really exciting. There was electricity in the air.

Well, not really. If there was electricity in the air, we would have been electrocuted.

Anyway, the Halloween Monster reached up and removed his head. And you'll never believe in a million hundred years who was inside the costume.

I'm not going to tell you.

Okay, okay, I'll tell you. But you have to read the next chapter to find out. So nah-nah-nah boo-boo on you!

If you've read a bunch of My Weird School books, you probably think you know the true identity of the Halloween Monster. You probably think it's Mr. Klutz, our school principal, playing a trick on me and the gang. Or maybe you think it's

Dr. Carbles, the president of the Board of Education. He is a mean guy. Or it could be Officer Spence, our security guard. Or maybe you think it's Mr. Docker, our science teacher.

Well, you're wrong! It's not *any* of those people. And it's not George Washington or Christopher Columbus or Lady Gaga either. Nice try though.

Slowly, the Halloween Monster removed the head of his costume. We could hardly believe who was inside.

"Mayor Hubble!" everybody shouted.

Mayor Hubble used to be the mayor of our town. Then he was arrested for stealing fake gold and silver that our

groundskeeper, Mr. Burke, hid in the playground. The mayor was sent to jail, but he got time off for good behavior. After that he was sent to jail again when he got caught trespassing and stealing signs from people's lawns.

"I thought you were in jail," said Mrs. Yonkers.

"I got time off for good behavior," said Mayor Hubble.

"You're supposed to be a role model for young people," scolded Mrs. Yonkers. "Instead, you're going around stealing their candy and trying to take over the world. You should be ashamed of yourself!"

The policemen slapped handcuffs on Mayor Hubble and started dragging him away.

"Wait!" Mayor Hubble yelled. "I can explain!"

"Let's hear it," said Mrs. Yonkers. "I want to know why you wanted to steal my invention so badly."

"Okay, I'll tell you the truth," said Mayor Hubble. "My grandfather . . . was Edwin Hubble."

For a moment there was silence. You could hear a pin drop.*

"Who's Edwin Hubble?" I finally asked.

---

*That is, if anybody dropped a bunch of pins. But why would they do that? Who carries pins around with them anyway?

"He's the guy who proved that the universe is expanding," Andrea said. "Weren't you listening, Arlo?"

"Your *face* wasn't listening," I said.

"When I was a little boy, Grandpa Hubble told me his theory about the universe expanding," Mayor Hubble said quietly. "He said that someday he would build a machine that would speed up the process and make things bigger. But he never did. For years I've tried to build such a machine myself. It was my lifetime goal. But I couldn't do it. And now it's too late. You made the machine. You'll get all the glory. My life is ruined."

Mayor Hubble started weeping and

sobbing. What a crybaby! That guy is worse than Emily.

"Take him away, boys," Mrs. Yonkers told the policemen.

"B-but . . . ," said Mayor Hubble.

Everybody started giggling because the mayor said "but," which sounds just like "butt" except it's missing a *t*.

"I'm not a crook!" Mayor Hubble yelled as the policemen dragged him away. "I'm an honest man! I'll be back, I promise you that! I'll be back!"

Well, that's pretty much what happened. It was a weird Halloween night, that's for sure. We all piled into Mrs. Yonkers's minivan, and she gave us rides home. The policemen took Mayor Hubble away in the back of the patrol car.

Maybe he'll go to jail for good this time. Maybe my mom will let me eat candy on October 30 next year. Maybe I'll find out who TP'd my house. Maybe Ryan and I will go bird-watching. Maybe we'll find out what a cognito is. Maybe Billy will stop parading around in his underwear. Maybe some talking penguins will take me to Antarctica with them. Maybe I'll paint some pictures with the pigments of my imagination. Maybe grown-ups will stop saying blah blah blah blah all the time. Maybe Mrs. Yonkers will win

the No Bell Prize for inventing the Micro-Mole 4000 Expandinator. Maybe if I can convince my parents that the universe is expanding, they'll increase my allowance.

But it won't be easy!

- Professor A.J.'s Weird Halloween Facts
- Fun Games and Weird-Word Puzzles
- My Weird School Trivia Questions
- The World of Dan Gutman Checklist

PROFESSOR A.J.'S WEIRD HALLOWEEN FACTS

Howdy, My Weird School readers! Professor A.J. here. I'm going to tell you a bunch of stuff you probably don't know about Halloween. Because it's really important for you to learn stuff so you won't grow up to be a dumbhead like certain people I know (Andrea).

Okay, here goes. . . .

Halloween started about a million hundred years ago when aliens from outer space landed in Hershey, Pennsylvania. They showed up with these huge pillowcases and shouted "TRICK OR TREAT" into bullhorns. They said we had to give up all the candy on Earth or they were going to blow up the Hershey factory.

Okay, I made that up. Here's some true stuff about Halloween that I bet you didn't know. . . .

FACT:

—The largest pumpkin in the history of the world was 1,810 pounds.

Wow! That pumpkin should go on Weight Watchers. It worked for my mom.

FACT:

—Ninety percent of parents sneak Halloween candy from their kids.

That's for sure. Last year I got a bunch of Tootsie Rolls on Halloween night, but the next day they were all gone from my bowl of candy. My dad said he didn't eat them, but I know he was lying because I found the wrappers in his garbage can.

FACT:

—Americans spend $310 million a year on costumes for their pets.

What a waste of money. You don't have to spend money to dress up your pet. Sometimes, for the fun of it, we put my underwear on my cat, and he runs around the house like that. It doesn't cost a dime.

FACT:

—Everyone knows that normally, seeing a black cat means you'll have bad luck. But on Halloween, it's also believed you'll have bad luck if you see a *white* cat.

And if you see a killer whale in your bathtub, you'll have bad luck no matter what night of the year it is.

FACT:

—If the top of your head itches on Halloween, that means you might have good luck in the next year.

Either that, or you'll have head lice in the next year.

FACT:

—Trick-or-treating may have come from the ancient Celtic tradition of putting out treats and food for unwelcome spirits who roamed the streets during Samhain, a sacred festival that marked the end of the Celtic year.

Wow, and I thought the Celtics just played basketball.

FACT:

—Jack-o'-lanterns are based on an Irish tradition in which candles were placed in hollowed-out turnips to keep away evil spirits and ghosts during the Samhain holiday.

Turnips are weird. Those things definitely don't look like food.

FACT:

—Surveys suggest that 30 percent of kids sort their candy when returning home from trick-or-treating.

I always put my candy in alphabetical order. That's the first rule of being a kid.

FACT:

—Chocolate bars are typically considered the most popular trick-or-treat candy.

I love chocolate bars. You know what I hate? Licorice. That stuff is nasty. I ate a piece once, and I thought I was gonna die. I also hate it when a helicopter lands on my head.

There's a lot more stuff you could learn about Halloween, but learning stuff is boring. I'd rather go out trick-or-treating so I can get more candy and eat it. See ya!

MYSTERY MAZE!

Directions: Help A.J. and his friends find their way to the Haunted House. Be careful! There are some spooky, scary creatures waiting to jump out at you along the way!

MONSTER MATCH

Directions: Each of the words in the list below matches one of the words in the circle. See if you can pair them up!

1. Trick or → ______________
2. Candy → ______________
3. Pirate → ______________
4. Graveyard → ______________
5. Witch → ______________
6. Werewolf → ______________
7. Full → ______________
8. Black → ______________

Moon Corn

Broomstick Howl

Treat Coffin

Ship Cat

WACKY-WORD STORY TIME!

Directions: Before you read the story, fill in each blank with a word that fits the description next to it. ONLY after you've filled in all the blanks, go back and read the story out loud! Is it funny? Scary? Or just really weird!?

On Halloween night, A.J. and his friends, ______ [*person's name*] and ____________ [*famous person's name*] set out to do some _______ [*verb*]-or-treating. They wanted to fill their bags with tons of delicious ______ [*plural noun*]. They saw all kinds of spooky costumes along the way, like a _____ [*noun*] and even a _____ [*something you find on the beach*]! At each house they would ____ [*verb*] at the door and _____ [*verb*] for some candy! Finally, they came to an old house that was scary and ______ [*adjective*]. As they ______ [*adverb*] walked toward the door, all kinds of _____ [*plural noun*] came flying past them, and everyone screamed! The sky got _____ [*adjective*], and A.J. and his friends ______ [*past-tense verb*] in fear! They walked up the front steps. Just as they were about to ring the doorbell, "_____" [*your favorite song*] started playing from inside the house! Something dangerous was inside, but they had come too far to turn around. Everyone wished they could just go to ______ [*place*] and _______ [*verb*]. All of a sudden, the door opened, and the owner came out of the dark house. It wasn't anyone scary at all! It was ______ [*teacher's name*]!!!

PRETEND PICTURE

Directions: The picture on the right is trying to "dress up" like the picture on the left! However, it looks as if the picture on the right made a few mistakes. See if you can find all the differences between the two pictures! [Hint: there are ten!]

MY WeiRd SchOOL Special
It's HalloWeen I'm Turning Green!
extras
GaMes!
PuZZLes!
aND MORe!
Dan Gutsman
Pictures by
Jim Paillot

WEIRD-WORD SEARCH

Directions: There are ten Halloween-themed words hiding in this messy jumble of letters! Can you find them all?

CANDY PUMPKIN HALLOWEEN
GHOST TRICK OR TREAT
COSTUME SWEETS MUMMY
WITCH VAMPIRE

O E S W E E T S K C A N T G R
K R M K Z Z K Q O N A R G D N
M I U U J L E S S H I N N H W
Q P R O T H M Q C C K I D J I
V M O K I S D Z K B K T Y Y T
P A N S J W O O E P O M W Q C
D V D V Y U R C M R A F V I H
T F K F U T O U F J V Z G V K
K P E V R X P Z G B B H B X T
G N E E W O L L A H O G I U O
F E A I T K P L Q S F X J P G
Y T V O U P S V T L G Y R L Z
S R S R T U I K Y D M H K R J
I L N M P Z T C V I U B Z X J
W G Y M M U M K I V F I J P K

WORDS AND WITCHCRAFT

Directions: Words can do weird things. See how many smaller words you can make from the letters in these bigger words. Try to come up with at least ten smaller words for each!

WEIRD SCHOOL

1. **CLOSE**
2. **DISH**
3. **COLOR**

Now it's your turn to work some magic!

GRAVEYARD	HAUNTED HOUSE	HALLOWEEN

INVISIBLE IMAGES

Directions: There are two pictures on these pages, but they are magically invisible! Connect the dots in number order until you reveal each invisible image! Then color the pictures in any way you'd like!

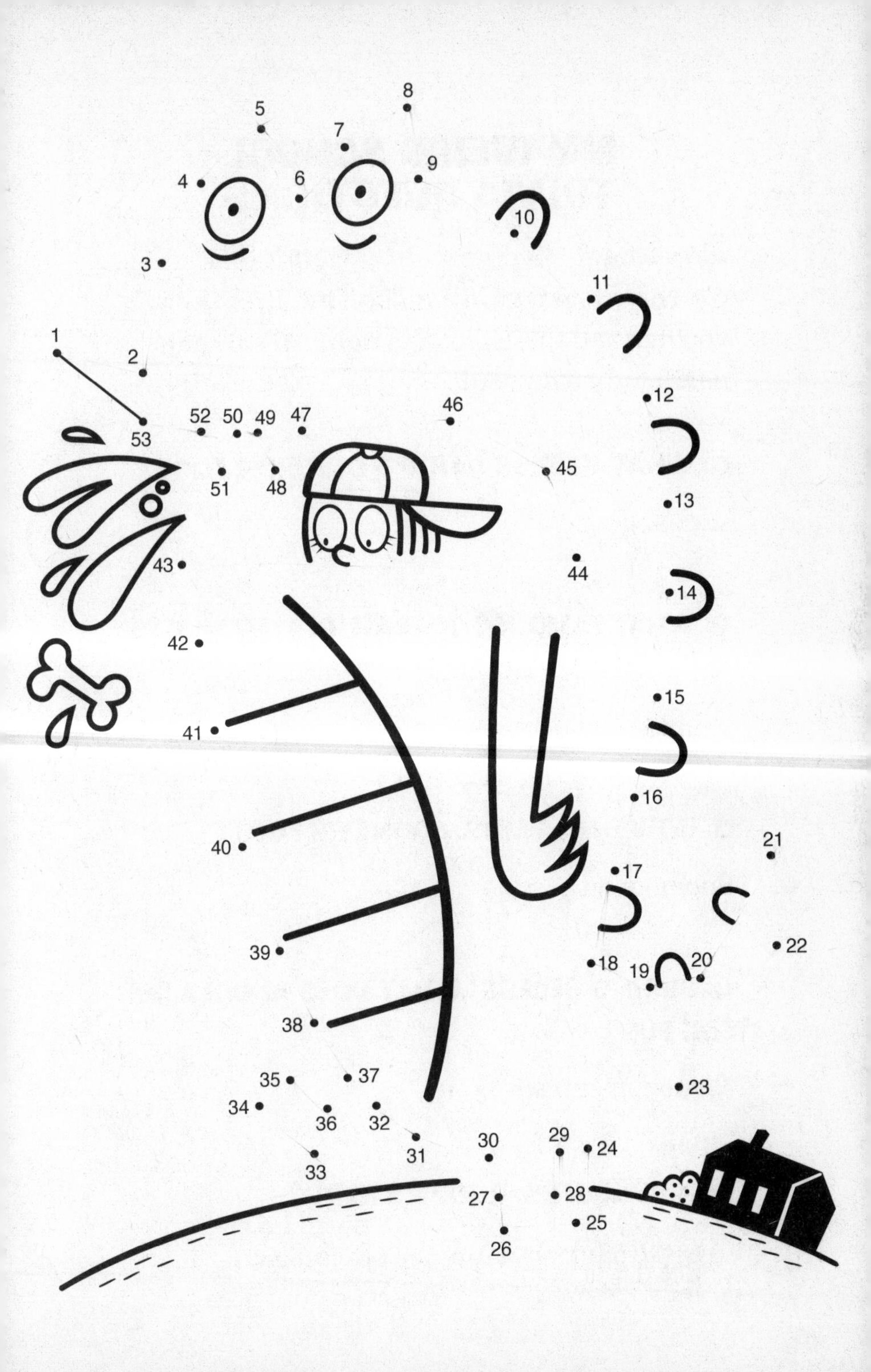

MY WEIRD SCHOOL TRIVIA QUESTIONS

There's no way in a million hundred years you'll get all these answers right. So nah-nah-nah boo-boo on you!

Q: WHAT IS MISS DAISY'S FAVORITE FOOD?

A: Bonbons

Q: WHAT FAMOUS FOOTBALL PLAYER VISITS ELLA MENTRY SCHOOL?

A: Boomer Wiggins

Q: HOW BIG IS MRS. COONEY'S FOOT?

A: One foot long

Q: DURING RECESS, WHAT DOES ANDREA DO FOR FUN?

A: Reads the dictionary

Q: WHO IS MRS. ROOPY'S HERO?

A: Melvil Dewey,
inventor of the Dewey Decimal System

Q: WHAT MUSICAL INSTRUMENT DOES MR. HYNDE PLAY?

A: Turntable

Q: WHAT DO THEY EAT IN EGYPT?

A: Food pyramids

Q: WHY DOES A.J.'S FAMILY EAT IN FRONT OF THE TV?

A: Because there's no room behind the TV

Q: ACCORDING TO MRS. COONEY, WHAT CURES ANY SICKNESS?

A: Licking your elbow

Q: WHY DOESN'T A.J. PICK HIS NOSE?

A: He doesn't want to pull his brain out.

Q: WHY DID MR. DOCKER MAKE A CLOCK OUT OF POTATOES?

A: He wanted to see time fry.

Q: WHAT DOES PTA STAND FOR?

A: Parents who Talk A lot

Q: HOW DOES MRS. KORMEL SAY "SIT DOWN"?

A: "Limpus Kidoodle"

Q: WHAT IS THE WEIRDEST THING RYAN EVER ATE?

A: A piece of the seat cushion on the school bus. With ketchup.

Q: WHAT IS NEIL THE NUDE KID'S REAL NAME?

A: Neil Crouch

Q: WHAT DO THEY GIVE OUT TO PEOPLE WHO DON'T HAVE BELLS?

A: The No Bell Prize

Q: WHAT'S A WICHSAND?

A: A sandwich that has the meat on the outside and bread in the middle

Q: WHICH PRESIDENT LIKED TO GO SKINNY-DIPPING?

A: John Quincy Adams

Q: WHAT DO YOU CALL AN ANIMAL DOCTOR WHO DOESN'T EAT MEAT?

A: A vegetarian veterinarian

Q: HOW MANY SPOONS CAN RYAN HANG FROM HIS FACE AT THE SAME TIME?

A: Four

Q: WHAT DOES MR. KLUTZ HAVE IN HIS LIVING ROOM?

A: A half-pipe

Stumped? Turn the page upside down for the answers!

ANSWER KEY

MYSTERY MAZE

MONSTER MATCH

1. Trick or → Treat
2. Candy → Corn
3. Pirate → Ship
4. Graveyard → Coffin
5. Witch → Broomstick
6. Werewolf → Howl
7. Full → Moon
8. Black → Cat

PRETEND PICTURE

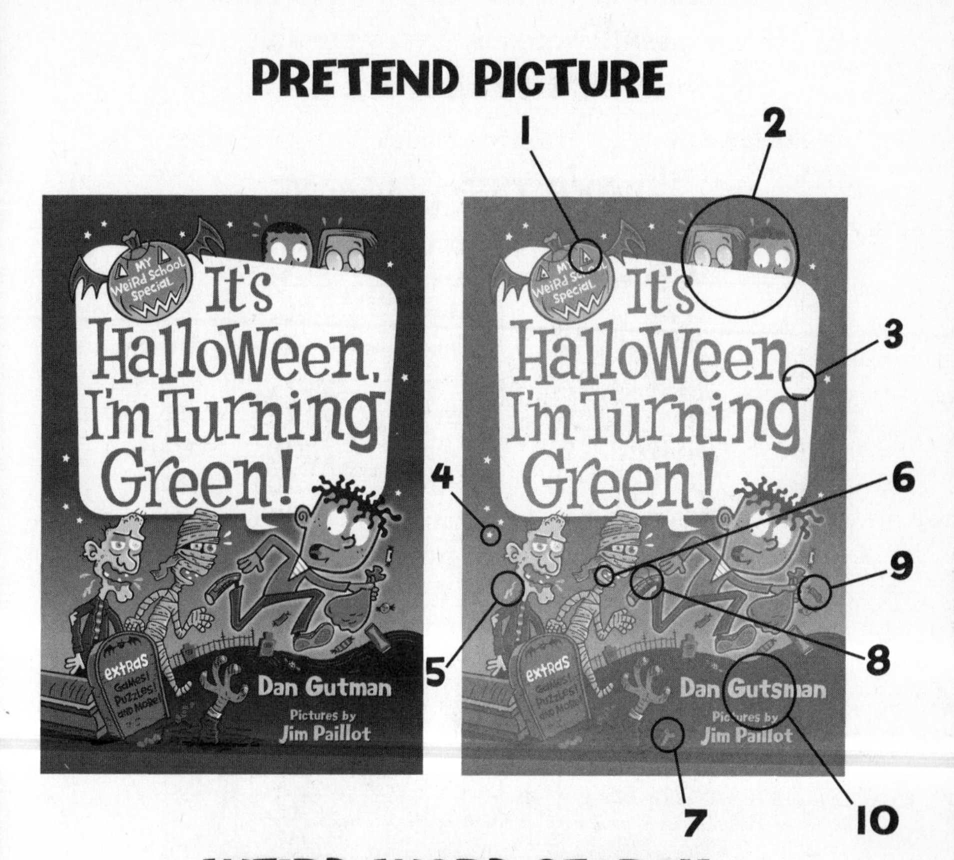

WEIRD-WORD SEARCH

O E S W E E T S K C A N T G R
K R M K Z Z K Q O N A R G D N
M I U U J L E S S H I N N H W
Q P R O T H M Q C C K I D J I
V M O K I S D Z K B K T Y Y T
P A N S J W O O E P O M W Q C
D V D V Y U R C M R A F V I H
T F K F U T O U F J V Z G V K
K P E V R X P Z G B B H B X T
G N E E W O L L A H O G I U O
F E A I T K P L Q S F X J P G
Y T V O U P S V T L G Y R L Z
S R S R T U I K Y D M H K R J
I L N M P Z T C V I U B Z X J
W G Y M M U M K I V F I J P K

WORDS AND WITCHCRAFT

Here are some words that we were able to come up with, but there are many, many more!

Halloween		Haunted House		Graveyard	
1.	Owl	1.	Use	1.	Are
2.	Wall	2.	Out	2.	Year
3.	Hen	3.	Hands	3.	Dye
4.	Whole	4.	Hat	4.	Read
5.	Lawn	5.	Shout	5.	Ear
6.	Wheel	6.	Tease	6.	Dear
7.	Heal	7.	Teen	7.	Grade
8.	Own	8.	Eat	8.	Day
9.	New	9.	Seat	9.	Very
10.	Hello	10.	Then	10.	Rye
11.	Low	11.	Aunt	11.	Gray
12.	Won	12.	Shoe	12.	Dare
13.	Now	13.	Honest	13.	Rare
14.	All	14.	Donate	14.	Yard
15.	Alone	15.	Thousand	15.	Gravy

INVISIBLE IMAGES

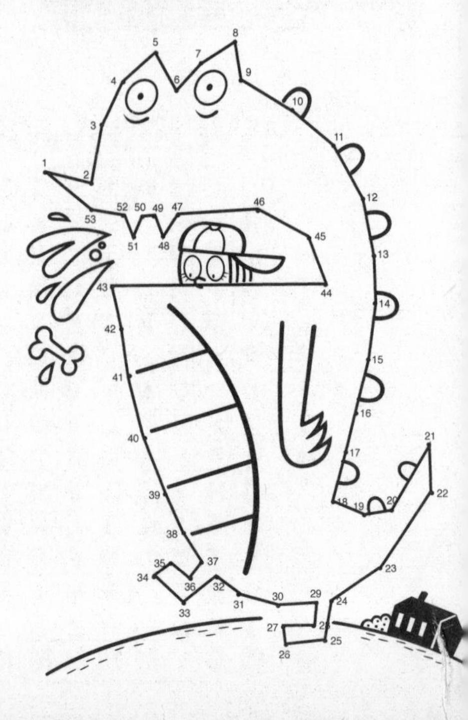

THE WORLD OF DAN GUTMAN CHECKLIST

MY WEIRD SCHOOL

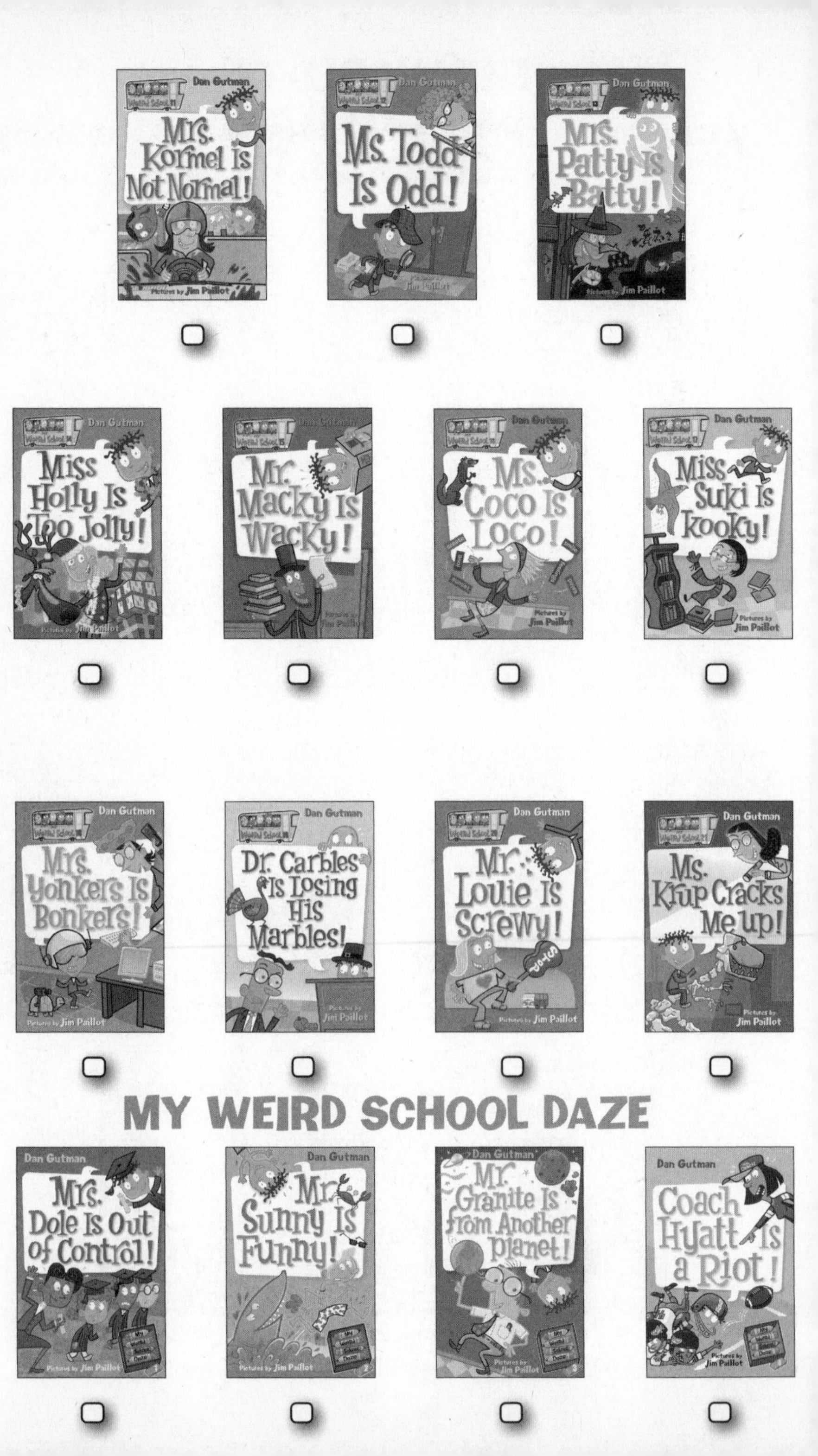
Dan Gutman
Mrs. Kormel Is Not Normal!
Pictures by Jim Paillot
Dan Gutman
Ms. Todd Is Odd!
Dan Gutman
Mrs. Patty Is Batty!
Pictures by Jim Paillot
Dan Gutman
Miss Holly Is Too Jolly!
Mr. Macky Is Wacky!
Dan Gutman
Ms. Coco Is Loco!
Pictures by Jim Paillot
Dan Gutman
Miss Suki Is Kooky!
Pictures by Jim Paillot
Dan Gutman
Mrs. Yonkers Is Bonkers!
Pictures by Jim Paillot
Dan Gutman
Dr. Carbles Is Losing His Marbles!
Pictures by Jim Paillot
Dan Gutman
Mr. Louie Is Screwy!
Pictures by Jim Paillot
Dan Gutman
Ms. Krup Cracks Me Up!
Pictures by Jim Paillot
MY WEIRD SCHOOL DAZE
Dan Gutman
Mrs. Dole Is Out of Control!
Pictures by Jim Paillot
Dan Gutman
Mr. Sunny Is Funny!
Pictures by Jim Paillot
Dan Gutman
Mr. Granite Is from Another planet!
Pictures by Jim Paillot
Dan Gutman
Coach Hyatt Is a Riot!
Pictures by Jim Paillot

Dan Gutman
Officer Spence Makes No Sense!
Pictures by Jim Paillot
Dan Gutman
Mrs. Jafee Is Daffy!
Pictures by Jim Paillot
Dan Gutman
Dr. Brad Has Gone Mad!
Pictures by Jim Paillot
Dan Gutman
Miss Laney Is Zany!
Pictures by Jim Paillot
Dan Gutman
Mrs. Lizzy Is Dizzy!
Pictures by Jim Paillot
Miss Mary Is Scary!
Pictures by Jim Paillot
Dan Gutman
Mr. Tony Is Full of Baloney!
Jim Paillot
Dan Gutman
Pictures by Jim Paillot
Ms. Leakey Is Freaky!
MY WEIRDER SCHOOL
My Weirder School 1
Miss Child Has Gone Wild!
Dan Gutman
Pictures by Jim Paillot
My Weirder School 2
Mr. Harrison Is Embarrassin'!
Dan Gutman
Pictures by Jim Paillot
My Weirder School 3
Mrs. Lilly Is Silly!
Dan Gutman
My Weirder School 4
Dan Gutman
Mr. Burke Is Berserk!
Pictures by Jim Paillot
My Weirder School 5
Dan Gutman
Ms. Beard Is Weird!
Jim Paillot
My Weirder School 6
Mayor Hubble Is in Trouble!
ANDREA
Dan Gutman
Pictures by Jim Paillot
My Weirder School 7
Miss Kraft Is Daft!
Dan Gutman
Jim Paillot